Amazon review:

Alice - a modern day ethics story

<u>M. Stuever</u>

I picked up this short book and read it in one sitting, just a little over an hour, and found myself laughing, crying and getting totally sucked into the story. Yet a day later, the ethical storyline is still sticking with me to the point of sending me online to write about this modern age tale of individual backbone in the face of corporate greed. Oh, the world needs more books like this...short, strong, compelling, but full of inspiration and hope that we not only can overcome the SYSTEM, we can change it and create a world where people count as much as profits.

Alice

A long story

or

a short novel

Sheri McGuinn

Durare
Publishing
Bullhead City, AZ

Paperback ISBN: 978-0-9855270-5-1

EBook: 978-0-9855270-6-8

HUMAN AUTHORED
Authors Guild
6125554

Table of Contents

1: The Arrival

This is the story of my mother, Alice McKenna.

You know her as the Rosa Parks of the Taxpayers Civil Rights Movement, because of the moment in August 2013 that sparked the Movement, the moment my mom said "No."

If you'd known her a few months earlier, you'd never have believed it was the same person. I guess it started back in March, when she got pink-slipped.

Frankly, my first reaction was relief that she wouldn't be teaching at the high school when I hit ninth grade the next fall.

It was as if God had smiled on me. My girlfriends and I could have fun in high school, without teachers reporting every little thing to my mother.

She'd been teaching French for eight years in our small school system south of Buffalo, but then they cut all the foreign languages except Spanish. They had to keep one because four years of a language is required for a New York State Regents diploma. They said Spanish would be more useful.

Besides, that teacher had been there longer.

Mom said when she first got her teaching degree she had six interviews and six job offers, so I figured she'd have another position lined up by the end of the school year. There were plenty of districts within an easy commute, and if we had to move, my friends swore we'd stay in touch.

But school was out, and Mom didn't have a new job. She'd applied to at least a dozen places, even in other states, and they only asked her to two interviews, close to the border with Quebec, where they thought French was more important than Spanish. But both of those schools hired less experienced—read that cheaper—teachers.

So the day after school got out in June, I helped her pack up her classroom and take everything home.

We were unloading the car, stacking all her stuff in the garage, when a yellow taxi pulled up in front of our house. A long-haired, scruffy old man in jeans pulled a dirty army surplus duffle bag out of the back seat and turned to look at us.

Maybe I should back up a minute.

You need to understand, my mom was perfect.

She always followed every rule. The only wild and crazy thing she'd ever done was go to a sperm bank for my other half. She said she was almost thirty when she decided that was the only way she'd ever have a kid.

Most people assumed she was divorced, so we let them think I had a deadbeat dad I never saw, instead of some guy who sold his sperm.

Anyway, in my lifetime, aside from that, she had always been very proper. If she'd ever had sex, it had to have been before I was born or while I was on an overnight at a friend's house, but there was never any reason to think either of those had happened. There had never been a man in her life, as far as I knew.

She was pretty enough; it was that stiff prim and proper teacher thing that scared them off. At least that's what my friends and I had decided. She never swore or used what she called "ugly" words.

But when my mother saw this scruffy old guy standing by that taxi in front of our house—well, she not only dropped the box she was holding but she said, "Shit," *as if it was something she said every day*, like someone who'd say it when they got gum on their shoe.

She put her hand up for me to stay put and started for the guy, shaking her head and saying, "No, no, no, no, no! No, you are not here. You never came here. Get back in that cab."

He opened his arms as if she was happy to see him but she took a step back with her hands up to warn him off.

"No," she said. "Leave."

"Could you pay the taxi driver?" he asked as if he hadn't heard a word she said. "That bus trip took too long. I used up all the cash they gave me on food."

"Who they?" she demanded.

"The social worker, the one who found you on her computer. Just like Orwell's *1984*," he said.

"1984," she repeated. "That's the year I got the hell away from you, Jack."

Jack! My grandfather.

Of course I didn't know any relatives from the sperm donor. But because I'd needed information for a school project, I knew Jack was our only relative on Mom's side and that Mom left home at sixteen and never looked back.

That's *all* I knew.

She insisted she hadn't had any contact with him since she left, that he could be anywhere. In fact, she'd made it sound like he was probably dead by now, though I wasn't clear why. Now here he was, alive and making my proper mother swear. I'd never seen her get so angry or flustered, and the more upset she got, the calmer he sounded.

It was pretty entertaining.

"Now, Baby Girl," he started.

She shouted over him. "Don't Baby Girl me! What are you doing here?"

The taxi driver rolled down the passenger window at that point and let Mom know the meter was still running.

"Do you want to pay me, lady? Sounds like this could take some time for you to sort it all out, and that could get expensive."

"Can't you just take him back to the bus station where you picked him up?" she asked.

"If you want to pay double the fare."

"I'd have to walk all the way back here, Baby Girl," Jack reasoned. "That doesn't make any sense."

Mom glared at Jack and pulled some cash out of her back pocket to shove at the cab driver, who burned rubber getting away from the scene.

"You can't stay. Why are you even here?" she demanded.

"Well, when they were ready to release me from the hospital, the social worker insisted I needed to be with family. You're it, Baby Girl."

"Why were you in the hospital?" she asked.

"It wasn't a heart attack," he said.

"What was it?"

"Well, they weren't really sure, is what I think. But they did a bunch of tests and said there was no damage to the heart, so it wasn't a heart attack."

I could almost hear Mom's teeth gritting as she pulled the answers out of him.

"Were you having chest pains?"

"Well, I got so upset when those cops came," he said.

She interrupted. "You were being arrested again?"

Mom had obviously forgotten I was still there in the garage where I could hear everything. They were talking plenty loud enough.

"I'd been in that house for years," he complained.

"What house?"

"In Garberville."

"You went back to Humboldt County."

Mom said this as if it meant more than she was saying, something negative.

"I'd been renting the same place for, I don't know, probably ten years. Then the owner decided to take it back!"

"You?" she scoffed. "You were in the same place ten years?"

"Well, Baby Girl, I'm getting up there, you know. Moving around gets harder as you get older."

"It's tough when you're a kid, too, bouncing from one school to another every few months, *when* you remembered to register me."

"It wasn't that often, and besides, living different places is more education than you'd get in school."

"Yeah, I remember. That's what you said every time you wanted to catch a Dead concert, or you wanted more sun, or you needed to get away from trouble with the law or break up with some woman. It's a wonder I ever learned how to read."

"I always made sure you had books, and I read with you every night."

"Every night you weren't too drunk or stoned. I could count the times you read to me on one hand."

At this point, he started rubbing his chest.

"Not true! You're not being fair, Baby Girl."

"Don't bother pretending to have a heart attack with me. I'm not a wet-behind-the-ears cop. I know you, Jack."

He squatted down by his bag on the sidewalk and pulled out a little bottle of pills.

"Quit faking," she said.

He stuck one of the pills under his tongue, closed his eyes, then took a deep breath and let it out slowly, all the while massaging that spot on his chest.

"You're not fooling me," Mom said, but she sounded a little worried.

"If you'll just call a cab and pay them enough to get me to the nearest truck stop, I'll hitch myself a ride and leave you alone."

"Fine," she said, pulling out her cell phone. "I'll do that."

Well, I wasn't about to let my grandfather leave without at least introducing myself, so I walked on out to the sidewalk. Mom was doing a search for a cab company, but she saw me and told me to go into the house. I ignored her. It was probably the first time I was ever that blatant about going against a direction from her, but hey, the guy was my only other relative.

"Hi, I'm Nina, your granddaughter. Are you okay now?"

His full smile was like a light going on.

I could totally see how he might have attracted women back when Mom was a kid.

"Granddaughter. Wow. Here you are half-grown, too. How old are you?"

"I'll be fourteen the first of August."

"That's almost as old as your mother was when she decided to be on her own."

"Jack," Mom warned, "don't you start on her. She's a good kid and I've given her a stable life."

"I understand," he said. "You don't want me around here causing problems between you and your husband."

"She's not married," I told him. "My father was a sperm donor."

Jack grinned. "Really?"

"From a sperm bank," Mom snapped. "Having a man in our lives would only complicate things."

"So now you know what it's like being a single parent," said Jack.

"I was *always* the parent," Mom answered. "Nina didn't have to make her own breakfast at four years old; she didn't get left alone for days on end at any point in her life. I've always arranged my work to be with my daughter as much as possible and *she's never had to take care of me.*"

"I did when you had the flu," I reminded her. "I even made chicken soup from scratch."

"You cook?" he asked.

"I can," I answered.

"Man, I'm hungry," he said. "Do you think we could convince your mother to let me stay for some lunch, at least?"

"Fine," Mom said. "Lunch. Then you leave."

Of course that's not what happened.

2: Rosa Parks?

Rosa Parks was a hard-working woman, so when she refused to give up her seat on that bus, her example connected with other people who were quietly trying to get along and make do. It wasn't the first thing that happened in the African-American Civil Rights Movement, but it was the catalyst that pulled in all those quiet people and gave the movement the numbers needed to make real change.

Mom's moment was the same kind of thing. That's why she's the one the history books talk about. People who were young or unemployed had already started shouting for change in the Arab Spring, riots in England, and the Occupy Movement.

Average working people were too busy trying to hold onto their homes and jobs to get involved. Mom was one of those quiet people. She'd lost her job, but she still thought like an employed person and she was busy looking for work. As the weeks passed without a job offer, she got more stressed, but her moment hadn't come yet.

The end of June and most of July, Jack was the target for all of her frustration. She didn't mean to let him stay when I took him into the house for lunch that day, but at some level she must have known it was inevitable.

3: Just for Lunch

Mom and I had stopped to eat on the way home from her school. She told me it was a special treat; until she landed a job we wouldn't be eating out anymore. She'd started being extra careful with money as soon as she found out her contract wasn't being renewed for the fall, so I enjoyed Denny's while I could.

It was like ninety degrees and humid now, and of course we weren't using the air conditioning because of the money, but I figured the old guy needed a good solid meal if she was really going to put him out on the highway. So I heated up some of Mom's homemade stew in the microwave while they talked.

"We'll feed you, then I'll give you a ride to a truck stop myself," Mom said.

"That'll be fine, Baby Girl. I told those people at the hospital you wouldn't want me around, but they felt better thinking they were sending me to family."

He sat down and I put the bowl of stew in front of him with a spoon and some crackers. Mom didn't sit.

"Thanks," he said. He took a spoonful of stew.

Mom just stood there with her arms crossed.

"I should have gone to Arizona in the first place," he said. "Last I knew, Jimmy Parks was still kicking. He'll let me sleep on his couch."

"You're still pretending to be a Vietnam vet?"

Mom was using her stern teacher voice.

"It was never pretending. You can call the hospital if you don't believe me. They wouldn't treat me if I wasn't a vet." He put a card on the table next to his food and went back to eating the stew.

"I will." She snatched up the card, thinking she was calling his bluff. "They won't tell me anything, though."

"Yeah they will. I signed off for you. Figured if I croaked, they'd track you down and you might want to know what happened."

"Decades of drug abuse will do a lot of damage," she said.

"I haven't used anything except pot since 1985," he said. "Haven't even had a beer since then."

"Because I left?"

"No. I had Hodgkin's. Figured my body had enough poisons in it without my adding any more."

"Hodgkin's?" I asked. "Isn't that like cancer?"

He nodded.

"It's a lymphoma, hits the whole system. A gift from Uncle Sam and Agent Orange. I beat it, but the chemo and radiation they used back then were pretty destructive themselves. When I had those chest pains, they figured it was heart disease from all that, but my heart checked out fine. It was just a spasm in the artery, but they said if it happened again and cut off blood flow to the heart too long, that would cause damage. So I carry the nitro."

"You're serious, aren't you?" asked Mom.

He looked at her standing there with the card in her hand. "Pull out that cell phone of yours and call them if you don't believe me."

She went out to the back yard to make the call.

"Are you dying?" I asked. I knew it wasn't polite, but somehow he invited that kind of directness.

"No, I got a clean bill of health before they put me on that bus. But I need to take care of myself and keep watch for other cancers."

"So why'd they think you needed to be with family, if you're healthy?"

"Because I'm old, and the home I'd made for myself got taken away from me. That left me pretty depressed at first. Especially being all alone."

"Why'd the landlord kick you out?" I asked.

"Damned greedy guy's making it a grow house."

My jaw dropped. I'd caught *Weeds* a few times at Mary's house. Her parents didn't pay any attention to what she watched. But that was fiction. We didn't know any people like that.

"He was going to grow pot there?" I whispered.

"Yeah," said Jack. "They went and made medical marijuana legal in California. You'd think that would be good for the farmers, but it knocked the price down, and it's still illegal to feds. They'll keep track of everyone until they get the go-ahead to bust people again. So growers are taking it indoors, out of sight, doing intensive hydroponics. It's more profitable, too. I'm not the only one who got kicked out."

I checked out the window. Mom was still on the phone, looking majorly stressed.

I'd heard talk in school that there was legislation to make medical marijuana legal in New York, but it wasn't happening anytime soon.

I still whispered when I asked, "You smoke pot?"

"Yup. Have my medical card for back problems. But really it's to help me deal with stress."

He looked out at Mom. "I could use some now. You know where to get any?"

"No." I couldn't believe he'd asked.

"Your mother brought you up to walk the straight and narrow, eh?"

"I guess. Well, she's been a teacher. It's in her contract that she has to reflect well on the school. She won't even wear cutoffs unless we're camping."

"Seriously?" He laughed. "Good Lord."

"So she wasn't always like this?"

"Like what?" Mom asked from the doorway.

"Uptight, Baby Girl. You won't wear cutoffs even at home? Probably don't skinny dip anymore, either."

"No, I don't." The cell phone was still in her hand. She put it back into her pocket.

"So," she said, "they say you could go into the veterans' home, but there's a waiting list."

"It's bad enough having to go to a vet hospital. I was drafted. I'm not going to go live with a bunch of regular army types. I'll sleep under a bridge first."

"They said you get disability."

"Yeah, but it's not enough to live on."

"Well, you can stay here a few days until we figure out an alternative."

"Why thank you, Baby Girl."

He went to hug her and she dodged it again.

"Just a few days," she warned.

"Sure. I'll get. . ." He turned to me. "What's your name again?"

"Nina."

"Nina," he repeated. "I'll get Nina to help me find a bridge for the summer. Then I'll head to Arizona in September; see if I can find Jimmy Parks."

"Nina, help him get settled in the den. I'll finish unloading the car."

4: Settling In

We only had one television; Mom was weird about that. She thought it was almost all a waste of time. I even had to promise not to watch programs online.

At least I had my own computer. It was her old desktop, but I'd put in some new components to speed it up, so it worked great. No, I'm not really a computer geek. They had a workshop at school on how to build a computer.

Anyway, the television was in the den, where I helped Jack set up temporary living quarters. I figured I wouldn't be watching much while he stayed with us.

"Does this thing pull out into a bed?" he asked.

"No, sorry, but it's comfy to sleep on," I said. "I've zonked out on it plenty of times when I was watching movies late. Or we have those really thick air mattresses that we use for camping, if you'd rather have one of them."

"No, the couch is fine. How often do you go camping?"

"At least half of the summer, usually. We've been to most of the national parks east of the Mississippi. And we were going to hike the northernmost section of the Appalachian Trail this year, except Mom's got to job hunt now instead. We were going to do part of it each year and finish right after I graduate from high school."

"Don't teachers get tenure in New York?"

"Doesn't matter when they cut the program. She's mad she didn't get qualified to teach in another area before this happened; they would have transferred her.

But that would have bumped someone else out of a job, so she'd have felt bad about that, too."

"What does she teach?"

"French."

He laughed.

"What's so funny?" I asked.

"Your mother started speaking French when she was about your age," he said. "We were living with this woman from Quebec. It only lasted a few months, but your mother caught onto the language easy as pie."

"She never told me that. She never talks about anything before I was born."

"She had a whole lifetime before that, Darlin'."

I whispered again, "She used to skinny dip?"

He whispered back, "When she was a little tyke, she hardly ever wore clothes and no one wore them for swimming."

"Even when she was a teenager?"

"What are you whispering about?" Mom was in the doorway and she didn't look happy.

"We're just talking about how much you liked swimming when you were little, Baby Girl." He sounded completely innocent. "Thought you were unloading your car."

"It was almost done. Nina, don't listen to his stories. This man is the biggest liar you'll ever meet. And you, don't you infect her with your nonsense."

"What do you mean?" He looked bewildered, but I could tell he knew exactly what she meant.

"And no pot in my house," she continued to lecture. "Nothing illegal, or you'll get a ride straight to the police station, you understand?"

"Sure thing, Baby Girl. I don't want to cause any problems. I'll just sleep here a few days until I figure out where I'm going. I won't be any bother at all."

"Yeah, right. Nina, take him to your room and do a search for this Jimmy Parks person in Arizona."

"Okay, Mom."

"And leave the door open. I'll be checking on you. No stories."

Jack had never had a computer.

"Seriously?" I asked.

"Played with one at the coffee shop a few times, looking around on it, but most of the news was about people I'd never heard of. Seemed like most of them hadn't done anything worthwhile for people to care about what they were doing, either."

"There is an awful lot of stuff about TV personalities and movie stars and musicians," I admitted. "You get the news fast, though."

"But how much confidence can you have in the truth of it? They've always tweaked history, but they can do it way too fast with the internet. I'd rather read a newspaper, something where they know what they said is going to be around for people to take a second look at it. Something that's harder to change."

"You can get news from around the world, though, and get their perspective on things. Our Social Studies teacher had us checking the BBC last year."

"Really? Well, that might be a good thing," he said. "So you think you can find Jimmy Parks?"

"I can try."

It turned out that there were dozens of Jimmy and James Parks in Arizona, but we didn't find the one Jack knew.

"I should have had them check while I was at the hospital," he said.

"He was in the military with you?"

"We were in 'Nam together."

"When's the last time you talked to him?"

"Ten, fifteen years ago. Maybe."

"He could be anywhere," I said.

I was thinking he could be dead, and I think Jack was thinking the same thing. If they'd been together, his friend was probably exposed to Agent Orange, too, and I knew that was bad news.

"When were you in Vietnam?" I asked.

"In the early sixties. I got out in 1967. Headed straight for San Francisco."

"That's what they called the Summer of Love, wasn't it?" I asked. "We had a sub in Social Studies when we were studying the sixties, and he told us about that and Agent Orange and a whole bunch of other stuff that wasn't in the books."

"History changes according to who has power."

"That's exactly what Mom said when I told her the teacher was upset his plans hadn't been followed! Word for word the same."

"Well, she heard me say it often enough, and she was there for the protests. She was a tiny thing, she may not remember much of it, but she was there."

He dug in his pocket for his wallet and pulled out a plastic sleeve. I caught a glimpse of a young woman with flowers braided into her hair before he turned it over and pulled out a yellowed piece of newspaper. He unfolded it carefully and smoothed it out on my desk where I could look at it. It was starting to rip on the folds.

"That's your mother," he said proudly.

It was a peace rally. The toddler he pointed to had tangled hair down to her waist and she was wearing shorts and nothing else. She was helping a much younger Jack hold a sign: Make Love, Not War!

"Did she do protests when she got older?" I asked.

"Nah, the movement cooled off once they finally pulled out. There was still stuff going on, but the fire had died. At least for me it had."

He looked sad, so I went back to the search for Jimmy Parks. When I didn't find anything, I suggested calling the hospital in California.

"It's three hours earlier there, so that social worker should be there. Maybe she can help you find your friend."

"It'll be long distance. I don't want to run up your mother's phone bill."

"It's a cell phone. You can call anywhere in the country. Haven't you ever had one?"

"No. Land line's good enough for me. Besides, they say there's a link to brain tumors," he said.

"There's no solid proof of that, and they've made improvements to the phones."

"And for years they said there was no link between Agent Orange and neurological damage or birth defects. You can't trust the government or big business. You've got to think for yourself, decide what makes sense."

"Well, I usually text with it anyway. It's nowhere near my head when I do that."

"Good. You don't have a regular phone?"

I shook my head. "We're hardly home, and we can always reach each other this way. It would make more sense if Mom would put us on a family plan, but she wants me to learn to use it responsibly instead of being on it constantly. My prepaid doesn't even have internet."

"Your mother has internet on her phone, doesn't she? That's what she was doing before?"

"Yeah. All I can do with my stupid phone is call or text, and I have to buy the minutes myself from babysitting money."

"I'm just meeting my granddaughter and here she is taking care of babies herself."

He sounded sad again, so I babbled on about texting and Facebook and Twitter and all the ways my friends and I communicated.

"You don't have to be an adult to use those things?" he asked.

"As far as the internet is concerned, I'm eighteen."

"Does your mother know that?"

"Yeah, she lectured me about not talking to strangers online, but she caved on the age issue because she knows that's how all the kids connect. She admitted that's important. But she insisted that I keep her on my friends list, so I have to tell everyone to be careful what they post."

He stared out the window and let out a big sigh.

"Does your mother have many friends?"

"Not really. Mostly she works and then spends time with me. It was cool when I was little, but it's kind of a pain sometimes."

"That's probably my fault," he said. "When she was little, she made new friends all the time, then we'd move on. Somewhere along the line, she started keeping to herself. I didn't even notice until she was gone and there was no one to tell me where."

I didn't know what to say. Most of what he'd been telling me about my mother was really weird and didn't fit with what I knew about her at all, but being a loner was totally Mom. After all, she even went to a sperm bank for me. But I'd never thought about why she might be that way.

"You and your friends do things together, too?" he asked. "It's not all electronic stuff?"

"Of course."

"But not skinny dipping?" He smiled.

I was glad he wasn't talking about sad stuff anymore. I grinned back at him. "No, I don't think my friends would do that."

"Too bad. It's a liberating experience."

"We'd better not talk about that anymore. Mom might hear us. Where's that card for the hospital? You can use my cell phone. We'll put it on speaker so it doesn't give us brain tumors."

The people at the hospital connected us with an officer who connected us with another officer, until we finally got someone who could help us. Jack had enough information for them to track down Jimmy Parks. Unfortunately, Jimmy was residing in a cemetery in Phoenix.

5: The Neighborhood

While Mom went online searching for jobs the next morning, I took a walk with Jack. He still looked like a hippie, but he wasn't so scruffy once he got a shower, shaved, and put on some clean clothes. He complained about the bus trip.

"It would have been more comfortable if I'd hitchhiked," he said. "But the folks at the hospital didn't think I should do that. . . So, is this a small town or a suburb?"

"Kind of both," I replied. "It's more separate from the city and smaller than most suburbs, but there aren't a bunch of people who've lived here forever. I think most of it used to be a farm until they built these houses for commuters."

"So it's a bedroom community? People mostly just sleep here?"

"And work in their yards and gardens. The houses in this area are all pretty small, mostly like ours, but then they all have big yards."

"Folks keep things nice," he said.

"Pretty much."

"Looks like your mother picked a good place for you to grow up."

"It's okay."

"Where do your friends live?"

"Way over on the other side of town. Mostly we see each other at school. When we can all drive, it'll be easier."

"No kids your age nearby?"

"A few ride the bus, but they keep to themselves."

"Why's that?"

"I think they're Muslim. I know it's two different families, but all the parents speak English with that accent like Apu."

"Who's Apu?"

"On the Simpsons, the storekeeper?"

"Oh, that cartoon. I've seen that a couple times. Never bothered having a television myself."

"Mom's like that. She'd rather read."

"Guess I didn't do everything wrong."

The red Porsche with the personalized license plate that said "I SUE 4U" went by about the time we reached the vacant house on the corner.

"Lawyer I take it?" asked Jack.

"Yeah. He moved in next door last summer. He's hardly ever home."

"Probably busy taking people's money away from them. He doesn't have any kids, either, right?"

"I think he lives alone."

There was some new graffiti on the abandoned house and the grass wasn't coming back.

"That place looks like shit," said Jack.

"It's been empty a couple years. Mom said it's going through foreclosure."

"That's too bad."

"There's two more the other direction. They've been empty even longer," I said. "They're worse."

We went home and I made a scramble. Breakfast is my favorite meal to cook. Jack helped and then went to get Mom. They were talking about the empty houses when they came into the kitchen.

"I can't believe the banks just let the yards die off like that," he complained. "Don't they know that hurts the value of the house, and everything around?"

"Why do you care?" Mom asked. "You never believed in owning real estate, did you?"

"I hate to see waste. There are too many homeless people to have houses sitting empty all over this country, left to fall apart."

"Having homeless people move in wouldn't help much," said Mom. "They wouldn't be able to take care of the houses. Ownership is not cheap."

"Well, something should be done with them."

"The banks will put them up for sale soon."

"They'll have to sell them cheap, the way they've let them go. That won't help your investment."

Mom looked at him like he was speaking an alien language that she understood, but she didn't expect him to understand.

"Don't worry about it," she said. "Even if they sell at a depressed price, the new owners will invest enough getting them fixed up to bring their equity back in line with the rest of the neighborhood. It'll work out."

She didn't know yet what the bank had in mind.

6: Meeting the Neighbors

I decided to call my grandfather Jack, like Mom did. Neither of them noticed. At least they didn't say anything about it. He didn't really seem like anyone's grandfather, if you know what I mean.

Instead of looking for a bridge to stay under, he started getting to know the neighbors. I didn't mind tagging along with him because I was bored.

My friends were all off doing cool stuff with their families. If Mom hadn't lost her job, we'd be hiking the Appalachian Trail.

It turned out one of the Apu families was Muslim, from Pakistan, but the other was Hindu, from India. Their dads were doctors at the same office.

There was a Hindu girl my age, Ambar, and two Muslim brothers a little older than us, Yusuf and Karim. One evening while Jack chatted with the fathers, Ambar and I sat in her backyard talking with the boys. Her mother kept an eye on us from the kitchen.

"I'd never have been allowed to have Muslim boys for friends if we were still in India," Ambar said. "And when it's time for me to marry, my parents are going to insist on a nice Hindu boy."

Yusuf, who was sixteen, laughed. "Our parents would be furious if they knew how casual we are at school with the American kids. They wouldn't want us marrying outside our religion, either."

"I don't know if I'll ever get married, and I don't even go to church," I said. "We celebrate Christmas, but that's because everybody does."

"Don't tell our parents," said Karim. "That's worse than being a Christian!"

"Definitely," said Ambar.

"So you girls are going to be in high school with us this fall," said Yusuf.

"You'll probably get Mr. Zeller for math," Karim warned us. "He's a complete burnout—he should have retired years ago. Whatever you do, don't correct him if he makes a mistake."

We talked for an hour about the different teachers and what high school was like. We were all friends by the time Jack finished talking with their fathers and said it was time to head home.

"Three years they've been riding the same bus and never tried to talk to me before," I told him.

"They were probably waiting for you to make the first move. After all, they came to a country where half the people see someone whose skin's a little different, who talks with an accent, and immediately they're suspected of being a terrorist."

"I'm usually doing homework or reading on the bus, too. I've been doing that since first grade."

"Well, they've had each other for friends. Though that definitely wouldn't have happened if their fathers hadn't gone to med school together," he said. "When India and Pakistan were split apart by religion, the lines weren't as clear as the politicians tried to make them. It got ugly."

"Ambar wouldn't be allowed to be friends with the boys anywhere else."

"I'm surprised they let it happen here," said Jack. "But maybe they figure it's unavoidable, and they can manage it this way."

Three of the houses we visited later that week belonged to university professors.

Jack chatted with the couples about new developments in stem cell research, the trend towards globalization of the economy, and the social resistance techniques of Gandhi. In the last discussion, Mr. Parker, a young professor of Social Justice classes, eagerly listened to Jack describing the Berkeley protests he had participated in, with Mom strapped onto his chest. He asked if Jack would be a guest speaker in the fall.

"I'll have to let you know," said Jack.

When I told Mom how much Jack knew about so many different things, she still said he was full of shit. She used that word a lot whenever he was near her, and they argued almost every time they were in the same room—about personal stuff or world affairs, anything and everything.

Jack's check came to our house the first of July and he insisted on giving Mom some of it for room and board, which was probably why she quit saying he had to leave.

She was getting more and more stressed about money and not having a new job lined up for the fall. She was on the computer all day every day, putting in applications all over the country.

After she'd accepted Jack's rent money, he told her, "I want to invite some of your neighbors over for the Fourth. I'll buy all the food."

"Why? You said you don't party anymore."

"I can still be sociable. Nina didn't even know the girl down the street, and they've lived there three years. None of them know you."

"When I'm not working, I spend my time with Nina." When Jack didn't respond, Mom got more defensive. "And there's been a lot of turnover in the neighborhood while we've lived here. Most people consider these starter homes. The Smiths next door are the only ones who've been here longer than us."

"Your doctor neighbors are content to stay here, there are some professors who probably won't ever make enough money for another home, and there's that lawyer next door. He's investing his money to retire young and travel. He has no plans to move."

"You even talked to the flashy Porsche lawyer?" she asked. "Did you see that license plate?"

"Yeah. His name is Sean Johnson and he's not an ambulance chaser. He sues for the little guy against big corporations, and before that he worked for the public defender."

"Really?" said Mom. "His car says he's in it for the money, don't you think?"

"He bought the Porsche because he could and he likes the way it handles. It's probably the last car he'll ever need to buy. They're built to last."

"I can't believe you're defending a lawyer with a fancy car," said Mom. She changed the topic before Jack could say anything else. "What should I make? The doctors may have religious restrictions."

"We'll ask when we invite them," he said.

Jack invited everyone over midafternoon, so people could eat early and go to the fireworks when it got dark. A few people had plans, but most of them said they could come over at least for a little while. So we had our first party.

When I was little, Mom would have me go along to open house nights at her school. I'd sit quietly and draw or something while she met with parents.

That was the only time I'd ever seen her spend more than a few minutes with other adults. I thought she'd be formal like that at the party, but she relaxed right away and totally got into being hostess. It was another new side of my mom.

Ambar and the boys came over with their families. The food wasn't a problem. Everyone brought a dish to pass, so they had plenty without breaking their eating rules. They were almost the first to arrive, but they left early, too.

"Holidays are one time it's easy to gather with other Indian families," Ambar said. "My parents want me to remain comfortable with our traditions."

The boys said pretty much the same thing. That left me the only teenager at the party.

The Smiths were there. They were an old retired couple. Sometimes when we were away camping, Mr. Smith mowed our lawn. They stayed most of the afternoon.

The professors came with their families, and half a dozen other couples stopped by for a while.

Mom didn't know anyone, but I'd done some sitting for a few of them. I took a babysitting course that included first aide and stuff when I was eleven, then put out fliers all up and down the street. I was pretty popular with the families I'd worked for, but I hadn't had any calls for months. People weren't going out. Since there wasn't anybody my age left at the party, I played with the little kids, hoping their parents would call me when they needed a sitter.

Off and on there was some discussion about the empty houses, with ideas for their use thrown around and concern about how they were trashing the neighborhood. Sean Johnson suggested everyone should sue as a group if the banks didn't put the houses on the market and sell them soon.

"Condo associations have done it successfully," he said. "We can form a homeowners association, if that's what it takes."

But no one really got into that much because it was a holiday. Overall, it was a cool party. Everyone had left by the time it started getting dark.

"Mom, Jack, let's go," I said.

Jack said he'd stay and finish cleaning up.

"But it's the Fourth," I insisted. "It's not the Fourth of July until you've gone to the fireworks, right Mom?"

"Jack can stay here. Come on, Nina. If we don't leave now, we won't get a good spot to watch them."

"But..."

"Go on," said Jack. He sounded irritated.

"You can hear them some from here," Mom told him. "Will you be okay?"

"I'll be fine," he crabbed. "I've managed for years without you, you know. I can take care of myself."

Mom grabbed me by the arm and practically dragged me out to the car.

"Put your seatbelt on," she said automatically.

"What's going on?" I asked.

"You know I told you I never saw fireworks when I was a little girl?"

"Yeah."

"That wasn't quite true. One year I made such a fuss about it, Jack took me. I think I was eleven. When he flipped out, I figured it was a flashback to an acid trip. They took him to the hospital in a straitjacket."

"He did acid?"

"Jack did everything. But that wasn't the problem that night. He has PTSD, from combat. The hospital told me. He flashed back to the war that night, and it's happened other times, they said."

"Will he be okay by himself?"

"I don't know."

The fireworks weren't as much fun, worrying about whether Jack was okay, but when we got home he joked that he'd enjoyed them from the bathroom.

7: Fireworks

They were at it before I got up the next morning. They had started quietly, probably so I wouldn't hear, but by the time I was dressed, they'd both forgotten that. I might as well have been in the same room.

"If you want to stay here, take the medicine they prescribed," Mom demanded. "I don't want to worry about Nina having to go through all that shit."

"I was fine last night."

"Hiding in the bathroom with earplugs, wrapped up in a quilt, right? Do you remember how many times I had to hold your hand and take care of you?"

"You're exaggerating."

"Once would have been enough, Jack, and it wasn't once. I thought it was all drug-related and it scared the shit out of me. I didn't know it was something you could have gotten help for."

"They weren't doing much for it back then. I've done therapy. It's not an issue anymore. I don't need the meds.Too many side effects."

"That's not what they said at the hospital."

"Doctors always want to keep you on drugs. It keeps you tied into the system."

"You're tied into the system anyway."

Jack's voice took on a hard edge. "I don't need it. If I ever give you proof I'm wrong, you go right ahead and kick me out. I should think you'd be glad I don't want to put any more chemicals into my body."

The outside door slammed and I went into the kitchen. Mom was sitting at the table leaning on her elbows, rubbing her temples.

"I'll be okay, Mom."

"My earliest memory is Jack holding me in a closet while he sweated through one of his spells. I kept patting his hand and telling him he'd be okay. I was probably all of three."

"Did he do a lot of drugs when you were little?"

"Jack did anything that came along. I thought it was normal. It was the only life I knew."

"Did you do drugs too?"

I figured I'd get in the question while her guard was down. It might come in handy someday. She actually answered me.

"He'd get so messed up that he'd pass me a joint even when I was little. I was probably ten the first time I actually took a hit. I didn't like it, though. It made me sleepy. I couldn't take care of Jack if I fell asleep. So I only did it a few times, and don't think that means you can try it."

"I know. You never tried anything else?"

"No. I babysat Jack on too many bad trips and I saw a girl O.D. on heroin when I was seven. I never wanted to try any of it."

"If you were so into taking care of him, how'd you decide to leave?"

"It was time."

"He's not a druggie anymore. I like him, Mom."

"I liked him even when he was a druggie. He wasn't good for me, though. I should make him leave before he screws up your life."

"We had neighbors over yesterday. It was nice. Jack did that. Don't send him away. Please."

"Maybe. I wish he'd take his medicine, though."

"The nitro? That's if he has chest pain, isn't it?"

"He's supposed to be taking Prozac."

"Why?"

"For the PTSD and depression."

"He did therapy for the PTSD, and he doesn't seem depressed. Maybe he was when he was sick and alone at the hospital, but that would be normal, don't you think? Wouldn't you be depressed if you didn't have any family and you'd lost your home?"

"The doctors thought he should continue the Prozac, Nina."

"A lot of people don't like taking that stuff, Mom. Kids say it made them more depressed or stoned."

"Your friends are on antidepressants?"

"No. I've heard other kids complain about it. Would you keep taking something if you thought it made you worse, or wasn't doing any good?"

"I suppose not. But you're spending so much time with him. If there's any problem, if he gets weird or depressed, will you tell me?"

"Okay."

"Promise."

"I will, Mom. I promise."

8: Who's the Grown-up?

Mom had had a few phone interviews, but no job offers. She was still checking for late-opening teaching jobs, but she didn't have much hope of finding one.

Her unemployment barely covered the mortgage. Jack's contribution helped, but it still wasn't enough to cover the bills every month. She started looking for non-teaching jobs that required French.

"Some of them are overseas," she explained at dinner one night. She was using her artificially perky voice. "Wouldn't that be an adventure, Nina?" She was pushing her food around without eating, though.

"I guess," was all I could manage.

Jack tried to sound neutral when he said, "That would be rough on Nina, moving right as she goes into high school. Isn't that one of the reasons you're still so mad at me?"

"We moved constantly when I was a kid, Jack. And I'm mad at you because I had to take care of you. I never got to be a child."

"That's not fair. You know it's not fair."

"That's what I remember, Jack."

"You don't remember hikes, playing on the river, or camping? Why do you think you like taking Nina camping? It was some of the best times we had."

"I really don't remember that."

"When I was in therapy for the PTSD, I learned a lot about how memory works. When there's a strong emotion attached, those memories stick with you, and negative emotions like fear and anger seem to be the strongest. But you still have the other memories; it just takes more work to pull them out."

"So when did we go camping, Jack?"

"I took you to Yellowstone and Yosemite and the Grand Canyon, and lots of state parks. Then sometimes when we were traveling, we'd throw out a tarp and sleep by the side of the road and pretend we were gypsies."

"We *were* gypsies."

"You thought it was fun. Your giggle was the most beautiful sound in the world."

Mom got up and cleared her place.

"I need to find a job. What do you think, Nina, should I take two or three burger-flipping jobs to try and make ends meet here, or should I try to find something that uses my education and gives us enough money to send you to college, even if it means moving to a new place - somewhere your worldview might be broadened?"

Jack didn't give me a chance to answer. He yelled at her. "You say I made you the grown-up? What do you think you're doing to Nina!"

"I'm right here, Jack," I said. "I don't care what you do, Mom. I can stay in touch with my friends the same way I do when I'm home and you can't give me a ride to go see them, or when they get to go on vacation and I'm stuck here with you two bitching at each other."

"Nina McKenna, don't you use that language!"

Mom was angry, but so was I. I stood up and slammed my chair under the table.

"Excuse me," I retorted. "I should have said I'm sick of all the shit."

I glimpsed Jack catching her as she came after me, but then I was out the door. I stayed away until midnight. Jack was waiting up instead of Mom, sitting on the couch with the TV on with no sound.

"She was really worried about me, huh," I snorted.

"I told her you'd be fine and that you'd come home when the lights were off."

"So she went to bed?"

"I told her I'd talk to you."

"And she bought that?"

"I meant it. I left the TV screen on to draw you like a moth."

"So talk." It wasn't fair for them to gang up on me. I stood there with my arms crossed.

"You haven't tried to get your mother to take you over to your friends' houses while I've been here."

"They're all away on cool vacations."

"Are you still in touch with them with all the social media stuff you told me about?"

"Not really. Actually, we've been kind of drifting apart since March, when Mom found out she wasn't being rehired. I'm in a different place than they are, you know? They're always doing things that cost money, and we're pinching pennies."

"Then I show up."

"I let them know my grandfather is visiting."

"But not all the details?"

"No, they wouldn't understand. They said it was cool when I told them about my sperm bank daddy, but it's always made me different, you know?"

"Different's not good for teenage girls, is it?"

"No, it's not."

"Is my being here causing the problems between you and your mother, or is it not knowing what's going to happen with her being out of work?"

I plopped down in the chair opposite him. "It's a little of both, I think. She's really stressed out by your being here, and by my finding out so much about her past. She's never talked about it, and now there's all this drama she went through. But not knowing what's going to happen is the worst."

"Would it help if we all went camping for a week, or maybe you and your mother on your own?"

"Maybe it would calm everything down if we all went, but Mom's too focused on job hunting and worried about money."

"I suggested it while you were out walking. Told her I'll foot the bill; I have some savings. Told her she needs a break from her job hunting."

"No kidding. She's so stressed, I wouldn't hire her." I hadn't really thought of it that way before, but it was the truth.

Jack laughed a little. "I was thinking the same thing. Should we all go or just the two of you?"

"All of us," I said.

"She's insisting on taking her cell phone with her, in case someone calls her for an interview or with a job offer, but she'll take a week off from hunting."

"Works for me," I said. "When do we leave?"

"Tomorrow morning. We'll head up into the Adirondacks, stay on a lake, and rent a canoe. What do you say?"

"Awesome!"

9: Family

That week in the mountains was like the eye of a hurricane. All the problems that were whirling around us—Mom's joblessness and money worries, my non-friend friends, Jack's health, the tensions between them, everything—all of that got left behind and we had fun.

Mom started remembering some of the good times she had when she was little, and she stopped looking for a fight every time Jack opened his mouth.

The weather was perfect.

We camped deep in the woods where we could hear wolves at night. The campsite was right on the water and the first day we rented a canoe for the week, from a truck that drove through the campground with them. We bought firewood and had campfires every night.

We did a little hiking, but no biggies. Mostly we kicked back at the campsite, swimming and paddling around the lake. We all knew what we were doing in the canoe, so we could take turns front, back, and middle. Jack and Mom talked and laughed about trips they'd taken down rivers in California. Whenever they got talking, I kept quiet.

"Do you remember that silly woman?" Mom asked. "The one who didn't know how to swim, and she was so nervous she actually made us tip over the canoe at least three times?"

"Oh geez, yeah. She was a sport about it the first two times, but she really got a mouthful the last one."

"And she was convinced I did it on purpose to scare her off!"

"Did you?"

"Hell no, Jack. I kept hoping someone would latch onto you for keeps."

"Except for the one who kept chasing me."

"Oh God, I'd forgotten her. What was her name?"

"Annabelle," said Jack in a Halloween voice.

"She had brown teeth."

"I have to admit, that was a factor in my lack of interest." Jack chuckled.

"That's when we lived in Humboldt, wasn't it? Did she follow us as we moved from town to town?"

"I didn't keep moving around for the fun of it."

"You were running from her!"

"Finally had to leave the state," he said.

"That's when we went to Yellowstone, isn't it!"

"Yeah, I told you the memories were there."

"We saw Old Faithful. How old was I then?"

"Seven, eight maybe. We headed south and lived near Santa Fe that winter."

"Then we lived in mountains the next summer, didn't we?"

"It may have been that year. My memory's pretty jumbled, too," said Jack.

"We went to the Rainbow Family gatherings when I was little, then stopped for a long time."

"I worked a regular job for a few years, do you remember that?"

"In California, on the coast down south. That's when I surfed."

"I liked that job, refinishing old wooden sailboats. Didn't even mind being tied down most of the year."

"Why'd you leave it?" asked Mom.

"I'd had enough of the ocean."

"It was after I nearly drowned. You were afraid I'd try surfing again."

"You weren't interested in going back out, but those friends of yours kept pushing, and you're right. I was afraid of losing you."

Most nights I left them talking by the fire. I'd go to sleep to the sound of their muffled laughter. But one night near the end of the week, I got wide awake when I heard Jack ask Mom why she left like she did.

"I didn't know you were sick."

"Neither did I, officially. I knew something was wrong. I hoped cleaning up my act might make it right. Things were getting better, weren't they?"

"I guess they were. Then we went to the Rainbow Festival, and you went off doing your thing again."

"I didn't find your note for a month. I even asked the police for help, but they said you'd probably gone off with a boy and what did I expect, taking a sixteen-year-old to a gathering like that. I was scared you were dead, until I found that note. Turned out they were right."

"I'm sorry it took you that long. I wanted to make sure it didn't get lost. I knew you'd pull out your box of books sooner or later."

"How'd things work out with that boy?"

"Not so good. Soon as the drugs he was on wore off, he dumped me at a truck stop. Said he was going home to his girlfriend and college. He didn't want our lifestyle."

"Why didn't you come back?"

"I didn't want it either, Jack. I wanted to be normal."

It got quiet then, so I peeked out and saw Jack holding Mom. Her shoulders were shaking, so I knew she was crying, but Jack was taking care of her, so maybe it was a good cry.

The next day, we took the canoe through a whole series of lakes and had to portage it once to make it a circle back to camp. It was a lot easier carrying that big metal canoe with Jack helping than when Mom and I had done stuff like that by ourselves. Jack called for a rest part way through the portage.

"Do you have your nitro?" Mom asked.

"No, I didn't want to chance getting them wet."

"Are you okay?" She was worried.

"I'm fine. Exercise doesn't give me any trouble. It's when I get stressed out that it clamps down like a Charlie horse right up here."

He thumped just below the collarbone on the left side of his chest.

"And I don't always need the nitro for it. It's a cramp, so I massage and do deep breathing and it goes away, if I catch it before it locks down tight. I hardly ever need the nitro."

"You should still have it with you," Mom insisted.

"Okay," he said. "Next time we're out in the canoe, I'll put the bottle in a plastic baggie in my shirt pocket."

"Good."

It was the best argument I'd heard—no yelling and they cared about each other.

We were a family.

10: Jack's Secret

We were a family, and I blew that apart the last night by being stupid. Before I went to bed, I asked Jack about the photo I'd seen in his wallet, the one of the girl with the flowers in her hair.

"That was Sunshine," he said.

"My mother," Mom said.

"How did you meet?" I asked.

"She was seventeen that summer, 1967," he said. He sounded like he was young and in love. "I was fresh from 'Nam and wanted to leave it all behind me. San Francisco was the place to do that."

"What was her real name?"

"Sunshine's the only name she ever used."

"What happened to her?"

"She wanted to have the baby at home, but after your mother came, Sunshine started bleeding. By the time we got her to the hospital, it was too late."

"So you brought Mom up by yourself from the beginning?"

"We all took care of her the first few years."

"I kind of remember that, I think," said Mom. "Was it in the country, with a tire swing and geese that chased me?"

He smiled. "You'd toddle over to that thing and stick your head through it. Your feet stayed on the ground, but you could pretend you were one of the big kids. Then one of them would get in it and hold you on their lap so you could swing."

"So it was a commune?" I asked.

"Not really. We were just a bunch of kids living on someone's grandparent's summer place up in Sonoma County. But eventually people went their own ways. When I moved on, Alice came with me."

I should have left it there, but I blurted out what I was thinking without stopping to consider what I was saying. I should have known better. I should have known it would ruin everything.

"Our teacher said 1967 was the Summer of Love when people hooked up with lots of other people. How did you know Mom was yours? There wasn't DNA testing, was there?"

"Your mother was my Baby Girl from the moment I first felt her move in Sunshine's belly."

Mom stood up, knocking over her camp chair. Jack got up and went to hug her, but she put her arms up to ward him off, like she had the first day.

"I should have known," she said.

"Why? What difference would it make? Is Nina's sperm donor more of a father than I was for you?"

"Did you get a blood test?" she demanded.

"No."

"Why not?"

"Because I loved you! Even before you were born, you were my Baby Girl. Sunshine told them you were mine. There was no reason for a blood test."

"They should have made you get one."

"They wanted me to, but I made them take her word for it."

"Why?" cried Mom. "Why would you do that?"

"Because I could lose you if anything went wrong, if they made a mistake. With Sunshine gone, they could have taken you away from me. I wasn't going to chance that. Sunshine put my name on the birth certificate before she died. They couldn't make me take a blood test."

He grabbed Mom in a bear hug. She pounded on his chest.

"I could have grown up with normal people."

"Or in a string of foster homes."

"No!" She pushed him away. "You kidnapped me, an innocent baby, because you needed someone to love you, not because you loved me."

"That's not true. You know it's not true. Think of all the memories that have come back this week. It wasn't all about me. My world revolved around you."

He reached for her, but she flapped him away.

"I need to take a walk. Just leave me alone."

She took off and Jack let her. Tears poured down my face and I curled into a miserable ball.

"I'm sorry. I'm so sorry," I cried.

Jack knelt beside me, wrapped me in his arms and rocked me back and forth.

"It's not your fault, Darlin'. It'll be okay. It'll be okay."

When I blinked the tears away enough to see his face, I knew he didn't believe it would be okay. He looked like his world had blown apart, and his face was wet with his own tears.

The ride back the next day was depressing. No one was shouting anymore, but each of us was pulled in on our own misery—Mom thinking how her life might have been different, me feeling like I'd ruined everything right when we were starting to feel like a family, and Jack looking like his heart was broken.

When we got back to the house, he asked Mom hoarsely, "Do you want me to leave?"

"I don't know what I want, Jack. Just give me a few days, okay?"

"Okay," he said. "Whatever you need. I love you. You've got to know that."

She made a gesture like she didn't know or couldn't handle that idea or something and went off to her room by herself. I started crying again. Jack rubbed across the top of my back.

"Quit being so hard on yourself, Nina. She was bound to realize it sometime."

"Why? It never occurred to her before. She could have gone her whole life without ever thinking about it. I screwed everything up. She's going to tell you to go away and we're going to move somewhere I don't know anyone and it's going to be just Mom and me again and that's not a family, it's just two people, and it's all my fault."

"No it isn't. I should have told your mother when she was little, or I should have proved she was mine. But I was scared the blood test would work against me and I'd lose her. It's not all your fault, Nina. Not even close."

"But my birthday is in two days. After that, she's going to tell you that you have to leave. I know it."

He tried to give me a hug, but I dodged him, ran to my room, and slammed the door shut. This was way too much drama to share with the friends who were already drifting away from me. I lived in a different world from them; this would only push them farther away. And I didn't know Ambar well enough yet.

I didn't have anyone to talk to about how my life was falling apart. That must have been how Mom felt when she was growing up, like she didn't fit in anywhere, that she didn't have anyone close enough to share her problems.

I laid face down and cried into my pillow until I fell asleep.

11: Uncertainty

Jack was in the kitchen before me the next morning.

"When your Mom comes in for breakfast, keep her busy for a few minutes, will you Nina?"

"Sure."

He stuffed a locking sandwich bag in his pocket.

I knew what he was going to do, but I didn't say anything. If Mom found out and it went the wrong way, I'd never see him again, and I didn't care if he was biologically her father or not. He was right. He was more family than my sperm donor.

Right after Mom came in and sat down to eat, Jack belched and excused himself. I figured he was going to get hair out of her hairbrush, and now he had an excuse for being in her bathroom.

Mom didn't notice anything unusual, but I took advantage of having her alone to state my arguments.

"At least you had a father," I said. "He may have messed up a lot, but Jack was there for you."

"I messed up by having you by myself, is that what you're saying?"

I should have known she'd get defensive.

"No. Maybe. Having one parent instead of two has some disadvantages, but it beats not having any. You probably would have ended up in foster care, Mom."

"Or adopted. I was a cute baby."

"Fine. Maybe you'd have been adopted. There's no guarantee that would have been good, either."

"I know."

"He loves you, Mom. You've got to see that. Please, don't send him away."

"Can I eat my breakfast without this?" she asked.

"I don't want to lose him."

"I heard you. Leave it for now, will you?"

Jack came back to the kitchen then, so I quit bugging her.

"What are we doing today?" I asked. "You want to play cards?"

"Actually, I have some things I need to take care of," he said. He turned to Mom and asked, "Can I borrow your car for a few hours?"

He'd helped with the driving on the camping trip, after she made sure he really had a license, and she'd been comfortable enough to fall asleep while he drove. She still took a minute before saying yes.

"Where are you going?" she asked.

"I need to go into the city, stop by the V.A., and run a couple other errands."

"Nina, go get my purse off my dresser, please."

When I came back into the kitchen, they stopped mid-whisper.

"Thanks," said Mom. She pulled out her last two twenties and gave them to Jack.

"Can I come with you?" I asked.

"No," he said. "I could be waiting at the V.A. for hours. It wouldn't be any fun. Why don't you see what Ambar is doing today?"

"Okay, fine," I said.

It wasn't fine, though. I really wanted to spend the day with Jack, in case it was my last chance. I figured

Mom was waiting until after my birthday the next day to make him leave.

Ambar was going shopping with her mother. They invited me along, but I told them I wasn't really much of a shopper. That was part of the truth. The rest was that I wanted to be close to home.

If I was wrong and Mom kicked Jack out sooner, I didn't want to miss saying goodbye. I even thought about trying to leave with him, but I knew that wouldn't really happen.

While her mother was getting ready, I asked Ambar what it was like to live in a foreign country.

"I don't know," she said. "America's not really like your movies, but it is a little. Having different customs than everyone else is difficult. You want to be yourself, but you also want to fit in, you know?"

"Yeah, I guess that's true for all of us, but it's got to be harder for you."

"At least we speak the same language, so that wasn't a problem, though you do all sound funny."

I missed that she was joking.

"What if you couldn't speak the language?"

"Oh, I think that would be very hard," she said.

"Yeah. My mom's looking for overseas jobs."

"Ambar," her mother called. "It's time to go."

"I hope you don't move," said Ambar.

I spent the day in the back yard, trying to read. I dozed off for a while, then woke up because they were talking in the kitchen with the window open.

"You've done a good job," Jack was saying. "Better than I ever did for you."

"You've been here a month, and she's crazy about you," Mom said.

"You know, there was a time you liked being my Baby Girl."

"Yeah, well. Did you take care of everything?"

"It's all done," he said.

"Good. You know this isn't easy for me."

"I know."

"Thanks for not making it any harder, Jack."

"We all need our space."

Then they stopped talking. I knew it. She was making him move out. But maybe he was getting a place nearby, though that wouldn't do much good if we ended up living in some foreign country.

12: Nina's Birthday

I didn't want to get out of bed the next morning.

I was sure Jack would be sent packing by the end of my birthday, unless Mom let him stay until the next morning. My life sucked.

The smell of cinnamon made me get up, get dressed, and head to the kitchen. Mom had made my favorite coffeecake for breakfast. Jack was at the table with a cup of coffee, waiting for the cake to cool enough to be cut. Mom was pouring milk for me. They looked like they were getting along okay.

"So, what do you want to do today, birthday girl?" Jack asked when we were stuffed with coffeecake.

It felt like a trick question.

What I really wanted was to go back camping and erase my stupid question that ruined everything. I tried for something close.

"The beach—we haven't been all summer."

Lake Erie wasn't the cleanest, but there were places you could swim and sometimes the waves were good enough to bodysurf a little. At least my last day with Jack could be nice.

"That sounds like fun," said Mom. "We can take an empty cooler and pick up some deli food on the way. Bring something to wear if we stay into the evening."

"I think I have a pair of shorts I can use for a suit," said Jack. "I'm assuming you don't have nude beaches here?"

I was afraid that would make Mom mad, but she took it as a joke and answered with a look and a shake of her head.

"Cool," I said. "I'll get the towels and stuff. Where are the car keys?"

"You get it out to the car, I'll load the trunk," said Jack. He got up to help Mom clean the kitchen.

I pulled together all the beach stuff and stacked it behind the car. I wasn't totally dense. There was probably a present in the trunk.

I'd put my suit on under my shorts and tank top and had jeans and a sweatshirt and underwear in my backpack. I got into the back seat with the cooler.

Mom and Jack came out together. She unlocked the trunk for him and got into the driver's seat.

"Did you remember the sunscreen?" she asked.

"Yes, and two towels for each of us, and the picnic blanket, and the sun umbrella, and a book, and my jeans and matches in case we stay to have a bonfire."

"And the cooler?"

"Yup. It's in the back here with me so we don't forget to stop and fill it."

It was almost as if those awful moments at the campground hadn't happened.

The only problem was, I wasn't sure if it was real or if it was an act for my birthday. Midafternoon, I gave up trying to figure that out and decided to enjoy the rest of the day.

Jack wanted to know if I'd ever been to the ocean.

"The Atlantic."

"The Pacific's colder, at least up north, but the waves are better for riding."

"Mom's kind of scared of riding the waves. She does it, but she quits as soon as they're big enough to have fun."

"Seriously?" He called over to Mom, "Baby Girl, you're still afraid of the waves?"

"Absolutely," she answered. "But I don't let that stop Nina."

"It's probably my fault she's still scared," Jack mumbled.

"Why?" I asked.

"The last time I saw her surf, she got held under so long she nearly drowned. I was so scared, I moved us inland right after that. She didn't have a chance to get back in and get over her fear."

"These are pretty big waves for here," I said. "There's probably a storm coming. You have to watch out for the undertow on days like this."

But we were on a sheltered beach. While you could feel the tug of the undertow, it wasn't strong and the waves were breaking so close to shore that you wouldn't be pulled far even if you were caught.

It was a great day.

We nibbled a little now and then, but left most of the picnic for evening. Jack and I pulled driftwood together for a bonfire while Mom set out the food on a blanket. We watched the sun sinking toward the lake while we ate.

"Remember watching the sunsets from the beach?" Jack asked Mom.

She smiled. "If it was low tide and the right month, we'd get crabs from the tide pools for dinner. Then you'd play guitar by the fire and we'd sing."

They were probably talking about the Pacific Ocean. I didn't want to interrupt a good memory, so I didn't ask. But when neither of them said anything more, I asked Jack about the guitar.

"You used to play?"

"Not too good, but everyone seemed to play guitar a little back then."

"I've been wanting to learn, but they don't have any at school."

"That's what your mother said."

I looked back and forth between them.

"You've been talking about that, about me?"

"Why don't you two get that fire started," said Jack. "I'll get the cake and presents out of the car."

It took half a box of matches to get the damp driftwood to catch fire, but once it got going, the wood dried right out and it was a nice blaze. When Jack brought down the cake, he only had one thing in his other hand. A guitar case with a ribbon on it.

"You got me a guitar!" I exclaimed. "Wait, who got me a guitar?"

"We did," said Mom. "I couldn't afford a decent one, so Jack pitched in. He picked it out yesterday. I hope you don't mind, but aside from some extra strings and picks, that's your only present."

"Mind? I don't think so."

As I opened the case, Jack told me it was used.

"There were new ones for the same price, but this one's better quality, better action, and a pretty tone. I tuned it for you. It'll probably need it again, though," he said. "New strings keep stretching for a while."

"Same as my violin."

"I didn't know you played violin, until your mother and I were talking about what to get you for your birthday."

"I had to turn it in, because I'll be in high school next year."

"You want me to retune that?" asked Jack.

I was holding the guitar like a pet instead of an instrument.

"No, I know how. I've done it on Mary's," I said.

So I tuned my guitar and played the few chords I'd learned from Mary.

"You're right," I said. "It's got a nice sound. Thanks, Jack, thanks, Mom."

I tried picking a tune, and then handed the guitar to Jack. "Play some songs."

"Man, it's been a long time," he said.

But he played around with the fingering a little, then started playing the old folkie songs from the sixties—all those songs you only hear at camp anymore. Mom sang along with him and I pitched in whenever I could.

The wind had picked up and a thunderstorm was blasting away out over the lake by the time we packed up our gear. We'd just finished loading the trunk when the rain hit all at once, soaking us in the minute it took to get into the car. But it was still warm out and we were all laughing about it.

It was the best birthday I ever had.

13: Letter from the Bank

As the days passed, it began to seem like Mom was over being mad and that she really was going to let Jack stay, but she still hadn't said so and he was still being careful not to upset her.

I wondered how long it would take for whatever he put in that plastic baggie to come back, but I didn't ask him about it. I figured he'd let us know if it worked out the way he wanted, if it proved he was Mom's biological father. If it didn't, it was better I never said a word to anyone.

So I kept my mouth shut and things were going along pretty smoothly. Then Mom got the letter from the bank.

"No, they can't do this," she said.

"Do what?" asked Jack.

"They're lowering the value on the house and how much I can borrow."

"You're borrowing against your house on top of a mortgage? Are you upside down?" Jack sounded worried.

"I'm not upside down. Prices haven't fallen that much here. But I need that home equity line to make the mortgage payments, until I get another job."

"So you're borrowing against the house to pay for it, and the bank's collecting interest on both ends."

"Yes. I know they're making out, but it's the only way I can keep the house right now."

"You might be better off selling," said Jack. "Hard as that might be."

"If I sold now I'd barely break even, maybe."

"Do they say why they're lowering the value? Have any homes sold in the neighborhood?" Jack asked.

"A couple," she said. "I've been watching. They weren't terribly undervalued. Not like this. I'm going down to the bank and talk to the loan officer. He's a decent sort. He'll be honest with me about this."

"An honest banker?"

"There are a few of them, Jack. Remember, I'm part of the Establishment now."

"If you say so."

14: Translation

Okay, you may not understand what the heck they were talking about. Jack explained the mechanics of Mom's financial situation to me. She was too upset. For a hippie, he had a very good grasp of finances and economics.

First of all, the term's fallen into disuse, but back then, being upside down meant owing more on your house than it was worth.

Mom had borrowed money (taken out a mortgage) to buy the house over fifteen years. She only had a few more years on her mortgage and she'd own the house and never have to pay rent or a mortgage again. Because she was paying it off in fifteen years instead of twenty or thirty, her monthly payments were high, but she'd have paid less for the house in the end.

Before she lost her job, she set up a home equity line of credit, which means the bank would loan her money with her equity in the house for collateral. Her equity was how much the house was worth, minus what she still owed on the mortgage.

Collateral is what they can take away from you if you don't pay up. She only had to pay the interest on the new loan, so she could borrow against the part of the house she'd already paid off to make the original mortgage payments on the rest of it—all from the same bank.

Now they were telling her that the house was worth way less than it was five months earlier when she set up the home equity line.

If we had to sell the house, that evaluation would lower the price we'd get.

If we stayed and Mom didn't find work before she'd borrowed her new lower limit on the home equity line, she wouldn't be able to keep paying the mortgage. The bank would eventually foreclose and take the house away from her, as if she hadn't already paid for most of it.

As for Mom's comment about the Establishment, that was a flash from the past. Back in the 1960's, a lot of hippies and other people called businessmen, bankers, politicians, and almost everyone who followed traditional paths the Establishment. It was kind of an early conspiracy theory.

Mom had been following a traditional path as a teacher with a mortgage, someone worried about what people would think. That made her part of the Establishment. Jack had never been part of it.

So Jack was suspicious about the letter, while Mom figured it was a mistake.

15: Jack Calls a Meeting

Jack and I wanted to go with her when she went to see the loan officer, but she wouldn't let us. She came home frustrated.

"He wasn't available. They told me to come back tomorrow, or to call the central loan office. I made an appointment to see him tomorrow morning."

"Maybe you should take Sean along with you."

"You want me to take a lawyer? A suing lawyer?" Mom shook her head in disbelief. "Are you kidding?"

"No, I'm not kidding."

"What happened to you, Jack? How much more Establishment could you get?"

"If they're pulling a fast one on you, he might be able to help. Think about it."

Except Jack didn't leave it at that—he went and talked to Mr. Johnson himself, and then he talked to all the other neighbors, too, and set a meeting at our house that night. Jack made sure all the neighbors knew to come with their lawn chairs and any letters they'd gotten from their banks.

"You're not the only one," Jack told Mom.

"You're overreacting," she said.

"No. This is just so people can share information, and Sean's going to let everyone know what their options are, that's all."

"What's he getting out of it?"

"He doesn't want his equity to drop, either," said Jack. "That's all."

"You're trusting a lawyer?"

"Baby Girl, there were lawyers getting hauled away in handcuffs when we demonstrated against the war. What matters is the person and what they do, not their title or job."

"I'm sure I've heard you rant against the whole legal system."

"Sure, and most lawyers aren't worth trusting. That doesn't mean every single one is a crook."

"Whatever," she said. "So, you've already told everyone to come, haven't you?"

"There were a few places with no one home."

Mom rolled her eyes.

Jack shrugged. "If you're dead set against having a meeting here, we can send them next door to Sean's yard."

"That would be silly." She sighed. "So, we're having a meeting. Or is it a rally?"

"It's a meeting. A rally's to get people revved up to do something. This is just for information."

"Good. Try to keep it that way. I'll make iced tea for everyone."

People started showing up a little after six thirty. Jack had told them Mr. Johnson would be there to answer questions by seven.

Mom wandered around offering the iced tea she'd made. No one would have known she was annoyed about the meeting.

Jack made sure he got contact information from everyone. I'd helped him figure out all the columns past basic phone and address—cell phone, Twitter, Facebook, all that stuff—and I'd found a clipboard for him in Mom's boxes from school. I sat down on a blanket with Ambar, Yusuf, and Karim.

"It will be interesting to see how democracy works here," said Yusuf.

"He's planning on going back to Pakistan as a reform politician," explained his brother. "He always sounds like a nerd when it comes to political things."

"Well, this isn't political," I said. "It's about the banks and people's loans."

"Anything about money is political," said Yusuf, "Especially when large organizations are involved."

I was about to say I agreed with Karim that his brother sounded like a nerd, when I realized this was about our home, and that Mom was upset that she could lose her life's savings. If that was politics, then I should be paying attention instead of making fun of Yusuf for being aware. I decided to listen.

Mr. Johnson got there right at seven and started by asking how many people had letters from their mortgage or home equity carriers that said their homes were being devalued significantly. About half of the people raised their hands.

"Which banks?" asked Sean.

They named two. The same one as Mom had and another one that he said was closely tied to the first.

"So we have to consider the possibility that these two banks have information that the others do not have as yet," said Mr. Johnson.

That made sense to me.

"I think it's a clerical error," said Mom. "I've got an appointment to talk to the loan officer tomorrow to straighten this out. Since it's not just my loan, I'll tell him there must be some kind of glitch in their system that's refigured our valuations inaccurately."

"I hope you're right," said Jack. "But if she isn't, Sean, what else could it be?"

"Well, their financial people could be looking at the economy and making projections. In which case, they'd be sending the same kinds of letters to everyone. We'd need to file to get that information. But with none of the other banks lowering values, and from what I've been reading in the financial news, that's not likely."

"You think they may have insider information that the other banks don't have?" asked Ambar's father.

"If those empty houses are legitimately dropping our values this much, I'd expect the other banks to be sending the same kind of letters within a week or so. We could do something about that, because the banks have let those properties deteriorate. They can be held accountable for that. Condo associations have successfully sued and been awarded empty condos. That precedent could work in our favor," said Mr. Johnson.

People made comments to each other that that didn't sound so bad.

"But if the other banks don't change evaluations?" asked Ambar's father.

"If the banks who have sent out the letters are the ones who own those vacant properties, they could be having them reevaluated as they stand now for their own purposes," said Mr. Johnson.

"Why would they do that?" argued Mom.

"It's happened in other places," he said. "An outside interest offers to buy a large number of houses at a discount. By reevaluating the houses prior to the sale, it makes the sale, and the loss the bank takes, look more legitimate."

"Then what?" asked Mr. Smith.

"Usually, the buyers borrow from the same bank to do minimal repairs, so the bank makes money on those loans. Then the buyers rent the houses out cheaply to keep them filled. Sometimes they get Section 8 classification so the government reimburses them for a big chunk of the rent. In either case, they're absentee landlords."

"That'll destroy our home values!"

I couldn't tell you who said that because the same kind of reaction was bouncing around the crowd like crazy, until Mom spoke up again.

"This is all conjecture. It could still be a clerical error, and I'm betting that's all it is."

"Let's hope you're right," said Mr. Johnson.

"Why don't we meet again tomorrow night and I'll let you know what they tell me at the bank?"

There were murmurs of agreement, then Jack's voice rang out above the crowd. It was amazing how he could do that, when usually he was soft-spoken.

"Sean," he said. "Worst case—if they are selling the houses, what would our options be?"

Mom glared at him for keeping the upset going and for acting like our house was his investment, too.

"It would depend on how far along they were in the sales process, but we'd need to take them to court to stop it, and come up with an option that was more attractive to the bank than fighting us."

"Well, hopefully that won't be necessary," said Mom. "Thank you all for coming. We'll see you here tomorrow night, same time."

It was getting dark before people finished chatting and headed home with their chairs. Sean was the last to leave. He offered to go to the bank with Mom.

"I don't want to go in with a lawyer," she said. "I really think that it's just a clerical glitch in some computer program and taking you along would turn it into an adversarial situation unnecessarily."

"Okay, but please, take my cell number, and if you need me, call."

She put his number in her phone and he left.

"Man, I'm tired," said Jack. He was rubbing his chest right under the left collarbone.

Mom noticed and didn't tear into him like I'd expected.

Instead she said, "Well, you were right that I wasn't the only one. I'll know to speak up for the others tomorrow."

"I think I'll sit out here awhile and enjoy the stars," said Jack. "Join me?"

"I want to write out my questions for the banker," said Mom.

"Nina?" asked Jack.

"Sure."

Once Mom was inside, he quit rubbing his chest. I breathed a sigh of relief.

"You were doing that on purpose," I said.

"What?" he asked, with that fake innocent look I'd come to recognize.

I rubbed the same spot on my chest and leaned my head back in my chair, saying, "I'm so tired."

He gave me a light punch in the arm. "You saying I'm getting obvious in my old age?"

"Yeah. I don't think Mom bought it, either. She just didn't feel like fighting."

"That works. How do we get her to take us along tomorrow?"

I already had a plan.

"I'm going to tell Mom that I want to learn how to handle something like this. That won't work for you, though. She really won't want you to go."

"I know," he said. "But if she's wrong about the bank, I want to be there for her."

"She'll be okay. Not to be mean, but she's been taking care of herself a long time."

"That's all the more reason I should be there for her now. Is there a music shop near the bank?"

"Yeah, there's one right across the street."

"They sell sheet music for guitar?"

"I think so."

"I need to get you a good lesson book. I'll get her to drop me off, then when I'm in the store, I'll realize I want you to look at them with me, so I'll come on over to the bank to wait for you."

"Mom won't like it."

"I'll keep my mouth shut."

I grinned and looked up at the stars.

Jack would sit there quiet? I'd have to see that.

It would be an interesting morning.

He handed me the clipboard and asked, "Can you get all this contact info into your phone?"

"The phone numbers, but I don't have email. I could put them on Mom's, but she might get mad."

"She wouldn't have time to delete all of them if you did it tomorrow morning, would she?"

"She probably wouldn't bother until later."

"Good. You'll take care of that, then?"

"Sure. But why the rush?"

"Well, she might want to let them know the results of her meeting at the bank sooner than tomorrow night," he said.

"I guess that makes sense."

We sat there quietly for a while. I saw a shooting star and silently wished for Mom to let Jack stay. Then there was another, and I wished for her to find a job where we wouldn't have to move.

Jack's voice startled me when he asked, "Do you have a large piece of cardboard I could use? Thin enough to roll up, but stiffer than paper?"

"There's poster board in Mom's school stuff out in the garage. Would that do?"

"Perfect. Are there any permanent markers out there? Wide tip?"

"Probably. Why?"

"I want to make something for your mother. A surprise. I'm not sure she'll want it, but if she does, I want to have it ready for her."

"Okay. Like a picture or something?"

"Something like that."

16: Alice Says NO!

Jack was cooking when I got up. Mom was drinking coffee and watching him.

"Special occasion?" I asked.

"Jack's battle food," Mom replied.

"Breakfast is the most important meal of the day."

"He always remembers that when he thinks there's going to be a fight ahead," she said. "When I was little, I knew we were going to have a long day, probably sitting or standing in the sun, whenever he scrambled up eggs and sausage in the morning. Other days, he'd forget about food until nightfall."

"Pour some juice for all of us, Nina," he said.

"Okay. What time's your appointment, Mom?"

"Ten."

"Can I come along? It would be a good chance for me to learn how to handle something like this."

"I guess so."

"Is there a music store near there?" asked Jack. "We forgot to get Nina a lesson book for her guitar."

"Nina and I can pick one up after the bank."

"I'd really like to help with that," said Jack. "There's more than one method."

"I don't want you at the bank."

"Of course you don't. Just drop me off at the music store."

"You'll be at the music store," Mom repeated.

"You can handle yourself without me at the bank. I know that," he said.

She agreed to give him a ride to the music store. He hadn't said he wouldn't come to the bank, though. Jack was good with language.

While Mom was in the shower, I loaded all the neighbors' contact information into her cell phone.

"She's going to be mad that I got into her phone without asking," I said.

"What if you tell her straight up that you did it?" asked Jack. "That might take the wind out of her sails. Tell her it's so she can let everyone know how it goes at the bank right away."

"Sure, so they don't have to wait until tonight."

That's what I said when she got out of the shower.

"People were awfully worried last night. This way they won't have to wait to find out it's a simple mistake that the bank is going to fix."

"You should have asked first, but that's a good idea," said Mom.

She was dressed up for the bank appointment, so I went and changed from cutoffs to good shorts and a blouse.

Jack was his normal self. He wasn't scruffy like the first time I saw him, but he wore his long grey hair in a ponytail, with jeans and a button shirt, tail out and sleeves rolled up. We dropped him off at the music store and got to the bank about five minutes early for Mom's appointment.

We'd just been called over to the loan manager's desk when I saw Jack walk in the door. He came up behind us so the man had to get an extra chair. Mom shot Jack a glare, but like he figured, she didn't make a fuss in front of the bank manager.

"What can I do for you today, Ms. McKenna?"

Mom pulled out the letter and handed it to him.

"There's been a mistake of some sort," she said politely. "I checked, and the last two homes that sold on our block went for more than their assessed value. Apparently, several of my neighbors have received similar reevaluations of their homes' worth. There's probably an error in your computer programming."

"I don't think so, but let me follow up on this and get back to you next week."

"No, you can follow up on it right now. I've been slotted for a half hour appointment."

Mom smiled her rock smile. She uses it when she's not going to budge. The man must have had a teacher like her somewhere along the way, because he understood that smile. He got on the phone.

"A Ms. McKenna is here asking about a letter she received. Her home has been reevaluated and she believes there's been an error."

He gave them the loan number.

"Oh, I see," he said into the phone. "So the new value was based on that? Yes, she said several of the letters went out to her neighbors. . . I will most certainly apologize."

He hung up the phone and held up the letter.

"You were right," he said. "It's a clerical error."

Mom turned the smile on Jack.

Then the manager continued to explain, "Those letters weren't supposed to go out yet, not until our sale of the vacant houses on your block has closed, which we anticipate to be within the next two weeks. But you really shouldn't have gotten that letter yet. I'm so sorry for the misunderstanding."

Mom stretched her neck before she responded. I heard it crack.

She was very quiet when she said, "You're saying that my home will lose this much value when you sell the houses you've foreclosed on, is that what you're saying?"

"Unfortunately, those houses do bring down the value of real estate in the neighborhood. However, the bank has arranged to sell them to a company that will refurbish and rent them. Eventually the values should recover."

"They were never put on the market," she said even more quietly.

"No, an international investment company has agreed to buy a quantity of homes to help correct our mortgage situation."

"At a price low enough to bring down the value of my home this much?"

"Well, of course there's always an advantage to buying in quantity."

She stood up and spoke with a voice that could be heard throughout the bank.

"You're saying that my home, the house in which I have put my entire life savings, is going to be devalued because your bank let three houses on my block deteriorate for two years before you even tried to sell them? Houses you didn't even put onto the market, you're just selling them wholesale to some international corporation that will be an absentee landlord in a neighborhood where people have put their very souls into their homes?"

Everyone was listening. She kept getting louder.

"You're doing this behind our backs and then telling us because of your actions, our homes are devalued, so you can put us upside-down and foreclose on us so you can sell our homes to some scavenger sucking on the bones of hard-working people?"

"NO!" she shouted. "You are not going to get away with this!"

She turned and handed me her phone. Her voice was quiet after her shouting. "Nina, get out of here now and use this. You know what to do. Start with Sean. Jack? There's an art store down the street."

She pulled all the cash out of her wallet and gave it to him, along with her car keys. He handed her the rolled up piece of poster board.

"I thought you might need this," he said.

She opened it and grinned.

"It's perfect," she said.

Then my mother went and sat down in the middle of the bank floor and held the sign over her head.

STOP STEALING OUR HOMES!

"Go Alice!" cried Jack. Then he guided me toward the exit. "Come on, we need to get out of here. Your mother will be fine once you get going on your part."

As soon as we were outside I grabbed his arm.

"I'm not sure what I'm supposed to do. I call Mr. Johnson, then what?"

"You twit and email and call everyone on that phone and have them do the same to everyone they know and invite them to a flash sit-in, that's what you do. I'm getting supplies for the posters. You lock yourself in the car and stay down low so they don't see you and figure out what you're doing. You can join us when you've run out of people to contact. But call Sean first and let him know what's happening."

17: Flash Mob

I did like Jack told me. I climbed into the back seat, locked all the doors, and slipped down to the floor with Mom's phone. I called Sean first and told him what was happening and what Jack had told me to do.

"Jack gave me a quarter for each of you last night, so you're covered by client privilege," he said. "As long as you're not telling them to do anything but show up at the bank, you're not breaking the law. Your mom may have to move outside, though. I'll get there as fast as I can, but I'm across town."

I sent an email explaining what was happening to all of her contacts, which included the neighbors and people from her school and her dentist and everyone she knew. Then I sent texts to all of my friends from my phone and asked them to get it going on Twitter and Facebook.

On all of it, I said to keep passing the word.

By the time I was done, dozens of people had shown up at the bank. I found out later that some of the customers who'd heard what Mom was saying before she sat down had joined in and contacted people to come, because the bank was doing the same thing with houses in other neighborhoods, too.

Jack was making posters on the hood of the car, and some kid was running them to people who were standing and sitting outside the bank. They all said "Stop stealing our homes."

Then someone started chanting it, "Stop stealing our homes!" And the crowd joined in.

Yusuf drove up with Ambar and Karim. Ambar took a sign. Karim started taking video with his cell phone.

Yusuf told us, "I called the television and radio stations. They should be here soon. Our fathers can't leave work, but they said we should participate as long as we are nonviolent. We're going to get it onto YouTube as soon as we get some video."

Jack gave me the last poster.

"The police may come take your mother away in handcuffs. I want you to be ready for that."

"Handcuffs?"

"Don't fight them, they're just doing their job, but if there are television cameras, make sure they see it's your mom being ripped away from you."

"Why won't they just tell her to leave?"

"They will, but she won't leave. She's making a statement for everyone." He put his arm around me and gave me a squeeze. "It's okay. Sean will get her out in no time. But she'll probably be a dead weight so they have to drag her out. It's passive resistance."

"Okay." It didn't feel okay, but I didn't know what else to say.

Before the police arrived, there were over a hundred people lining the street and shouting, "Stop stealing our homes!"

To tell you the truth, I was scared. Especially when the police did drag Mom to their car like Jack had warned me. I wasn't acting when I cried and went after her, calling for her.

But I didn't go after the cops.

There were a thousand people by the time the mayor came. The news about the bank selling houses wholesale was all over the internet. The mayor went into the bank, and the next thing we knew, the bank manager came out and talked to the crowd through a megaphone.

He promised that they'd set up a public meeting about the sale of bank-owned houses before going through with any sales.

When the bank manager started to hand the megaphone back to the mayor, Jack jumped up between them and grabbed it.

Before they could stop him, he faced the crowd and said, "Thank you, everyone, for supporting my daughter and all the other homeowners affected by this. Please, leave quietly now, but be sure you show up for that public meeting. Thank you."

Then he handed it to the mayor with a nod. The police were ready to grab him, but she motioned for them to stand back. The crowd was already starting to leave, even the teenagers who'd shown up just to be part of a flash mob.

Jack had that kind of charisma.

"My office will make sure that meeting is held and properly publicized," the mayor said. "Thank you for dispersing without incident."

Jack offered his hand to her. I couldn't hear what was said, but they were both smiling.

Once the place cleared out, I rode with Sean to get Mom out of jail. Jack came along behind us and waited outside for her. He was right, it only took a few minutes because she'd been quiet and polite to the police. I think the mayor had made a phone call to the station, too.

As we walked out, one of the cops said, "Thanks. Some of us got those letters, too. They're doing it all over the city."

Jack was leaning against the car with his whole face smiling and when he opened his arms, Mom walked right into his hug.

"That's my Alice," he said.

Mom pulled me into it and Sean stepped back while reporters took our picture.

18: Alice's Movement

It was almost dinnertime when we got home, but we were all too revved up to need food.

"I was so proud of you when you hollered out NO!" said Jack.

"You had that sign ready for me." Mom looked ready to cry happy tears.

"Well, if you'd been right, I was going to throw it away, but it felt like a setup."

"You called me Alice."

"Sure did. You went way past fifty people. You started a movement, Alice."

"Arlo Guthrie. You named me for *his* song, not the Airplane's?"

"Of course," said Jack.

Mom smiled. "I like that."

"What song are you talking about?" I asked.

"*Alice's Restaurant.* It was against the draft."

"I'm going to go check it out online."

"There's a movie, too," said Mom. "We can watch it later if we can stream it, if I can sit still."

I went to my room to look for it. We were all over the internet.

"Mom, Jack," I called. "You've got to see this."

They read over my shoulders.

There'd been demonstrations all over the country.

Some of them had gotten violent, but all of the articles talked about how it started with one woman saying "No" and sitting down. Someone in the bank had caught most of what she said to the banker on their cell phone. That and Yusuf's YouTube video were on all the major news outlets.

Yusuf had caught mom sitting in the bank and being dragged out completely passive. Mom saw his footage of me crying and bent down to hug me.

"You okay?" she asked.

"Yeah, you know, the first time for anything's scary," I said.

Someone was knocking on the door and Jack went to let Sean in. They came back to my room.

"The media's all out on our front lawn," said Jack. "They want to see you."

"They can wait a minute," said Mom. "I want to see the rest of this footage."

The television stations that Yusuf had called had documented the chanting, the police standing back, and an old hippie handling crowd control.

Wherever someone started to do something destructive or looked like they were going to get violent, Jack was there, talking them down. Some gang kids had spray cans. He stopped them before they painted, then they bumped knuckles with him and put the cans away.

"What did you say to them?" Sean asked.

"Not here, not now. One of them started to mouth off and I told him it was my show, if they wanted to be part of it they'd make sure no one did any tagging or broke any other laws."

"That's all it took?"

"Well, hell, they took a look at the size of my crowd and held out their knuckles to me. I met them with mine. That seemed to seal the deal."

"While I was in custody, the police told me you made their job a lot easier," said Alice.

"Well, it's always better to police yourself. It gets ugly when young cops feel threatened. I saw enough of that back in the day. That's why I was encouraging people to sit down—people are less likely to get violent when they're sitting."

"We're harder to move that way, too," Mom said. "That's what you always told me."

Sean said, "I did a little web-surfing before I came over. The class action lawyers are all over this. They'll stop massive purchasing, but they're in it for the money—they won't really help people come up with alternatives that are viable for the banks. We need to organize something better."

"We'll need to know how much they were willing to take for how many houses," said Jack.

I'd been following links while they talked.

"I think we've already got those numbers," I said. "There's a guy who quit the bank posting stuff online for everyone to see."

"Print off that page," said Sean. He looked at it and shook his head before he passed it to Mom. "It looks legitimate."

"That's insane!" she cried. "They'd take that little for those houses?"

"Bulk buying," said Jack.

"Nina, print off ten more copies," said Mom. "It's time to go talk to those reporters and pass out this information. And I'll tell them we're organizing to develop a win-win proposition for our neighborhood and the bank."

19: You Can't Get Lazy

That's how it all began.

With our neighbors, we started the Neighborhood Support Alliance, a nonprofit dedicated to protecting neighborhood values by providing local support networks. Each household pitched in at least five hundred dollars to get things rolling. Anyone making enough to use the tax deduction donated more.

The bank sold the Alliance two houses at the same price and low interest rate they were going to get from that international corporation, with minimal down payments. They donated the third house. Since we were nonprofit they could write it off their taxes.

Everyone pitched in to fix up the house in the best condition first. Then we sold it so we could build up the Alliance fund. We used that money to fix up the other two houses and sold another, which left us with money to set up the third house as a short-term stop for people recently made homeless, to give them a chance to get over the shock and figure out their options. Yes, Jack was a major advocate for that, but so was Mom. She'd really been scared we'd end up living in our car.

Once the houses on our block were in shape, we started working with other neighborhoods. We found out there was already a HUD program where the local government could buy houses for a dollar that the government had foreclosed on, if they helped low to moderate income families move into them. We'd help them fix up those houses, too.

The Alliance ended up having chapters across the country. Most banks decided it was better to work with the nonprofit than face class action lawsuits. Each chapter determined their own values. Some made the reclaimed houses into community centers or schools or homeless shelters, instead of setting families up in them. Sometimes houses had to be torn down because they were in such bad shape, and some of the Alliances used those empty lots to build playgrounds or plant community gardens. One way or another, Alliance chapters helped out people who'd lost their homes and worked to build better neighborhoods.

From the start, the Alliance was powered by those quiet people who had been focusing on keeping their own homes and their own jobs.

Together, those quiet people went on to deal with more issues where taxpayers were getting the short end of it, and it became known as the Taxpayers Civil Rights Movement.

The history books talk most about Alice McKenna, but I don't know what would have happened if Jack hadn't come to us that summer. He never did say anything about DNA testing, but I figure biology's not that important. Jack will always be Mom's father and my grandfather. And he's proud of what the history books say about Mom, at least until the balance of power swings and history gets rewritten.

Jack keeps reminding us: You can't get lazy if you want to live in a true democracy.

Thank you.

Thank you for reading this book. Please take a few moments right now, while the story is still resonating, to help others find it. Amazon's algorithms control book sales – the more reviews and ratings a book gets, the more often it pops up for people to see. The more attention it gets there, the more attention it gets elsewhere and the more likely it will find its way to libraries, too. So please, review this book on Amazon. You don't have to purchase it there to post a review and/or rate a book.

You can copy and paste the same review at Goodreads or other places. A review can be short and simple – "Interesting story." is enough for the review to be counted. Don't forget to give it a star rating.

Review links:
www.amazon.com/dp/0985527056
www.goodreads.com/book/show/18492916

If you want to do more, you can:
- Talk it up – encourage your friends and your local library or book club to get the book.
- If you do social media, post your picture with the book.

If you want to know more, you can check out my website. If you have questions, there's a contact form and I do answer messages.

Thanks. Sheri
www.sherimcguinn.com
sherimcguinn.substack.com

Author Notes

I wrote this book for fun, but there's a message to it as well. If you think that message should be heard, please write reviews to help get the word out.

The concept of using vacant buildings to house homeless people is not mine alone. In fact, there are federal programs to help this happen and banks have turned over many buildings. The resources listed on the next page are a good place to start.

Get informed, make a plan, and make a difference! Let me know what you're doing.

Sheri McGuinn

www.sherimcguinn.com

sherimcguinn.substack.com

Resources

A few resources the characters might use:

www.hudexchange.info
This is the central information center for the U.S. Department of Housing and Urban Development. Find out what programs are available to develop housing.

www.hudexchange.info/housing-and-homeless-assistance
Here they list resources for people who are at risk or already homeless.

www.hhs.gov/programs/social-services/homelessness/resources/index.html
Lists resources for homeless people including hotlines.

www.samhsa.gov/communities/homelessness-programs-resources
Resources for homeless people with substance abuse or mental health issues.

Also by Sheri McGuinn

All for One: Love, War, & Ghosts

Youthful decisions changed the course of their lives and estranged lifelong friends. Decades later they think 'Nam and PTSD are long behind them. Then the past shoves its way into the present bringing uncertainty and fear. By the end of the deadly month, their lives again change forever.

Running Away: Maggie's Story

Maggie's already in another state when they realize she's gone. Her mother's missing journal is their only clue. While Peg races to find her daughter before she's hurt or disappears forever, Maggie lands in dangerous company. Told in both voices, this is a stand-alone story, yet companion to *Peg's Story: Detours*.

Peg's Story: Detours

A novel that reads like memoir; one woman's journey.

Kirkus Reviews: "In some ways, the novel is a brutal cautionary tale, showing how one mistake can spiral into a life-changing series of events. In another, however, it is a moving coming-of-age narrative about a girl who discovers herself amid extreme circumstances. A nuanced yet plainly told novel."

Tough Times

"Stay together." Michael knows they'll be split up by the system, so he decides to take his young siblings to the white grandparents they've never known – because *his* father was black. While Michael deals with responsibility, grief, prejudice, fear, his first romantic relationship, and hormones, the police find his mother and label it murder. They think Michael did it, but the killer is stalking the kids. ***2023 KINDLE BEST OF INDIE BOOK AWARDS FINALIST YOUNG ADULT***

Discussion Questions

1. When do you first suspect there may be more to Alice than she presents?

2. Discuss Jack as a father – what did he do right?

3. Discuss the feelings between Jack and Alice.

4. Was it a completely selfish decision for Jack to sign Alice's birth certificate? Or selfless?

5. Jack has people skills. Alice warns Nina against them. Do we see him abuse those skills?

6. Nina is frightened when her mother sits down in the bank. Why? On what levels?

7. Alice was named after a song. Why does which song make such a difference to her?

My website has:

Supplemental Materials
Puchasing Links
A Contact Form
(ask questions or set up an author visit)
Media Resources

www.sherimcguinn.com

My newsletter caters to readers and writers:

sherimcguinn.substack.com

Review links for *Alice*

www.amazon.com/dp/0985527056

www.goodreads.com/book/show/18492916

Every review helps – thank you.

Thanks for reading!